SHOUTING!

by JOYCE CAROL THOMAS   Illustrated by ANNIE LEE

JUMP AT THE SUN HYPERION BOOKS FOR CHILDREN/*New York*

For Mary Ann Pollar
—J.C.T.

To my daughter, Joy; her husband, Charles; and my seven grandchildren,
Stacy, Shannon, Charles, Jr., Amber, Howard III, Antonio, and Marsha
—A.L.

Printed in Hong Kong
First Edition
1 3 5 7 9 10 8 6 4 2

Reinforced binding
This book is set in Scala condensed.
Library of Congress Cataloging–in–Publication Data on file.
ISBN 0-7868-0664-8
Visit www.jumpatthesun.com

The pink hat on her head
Looked like a flower basket
A bee could buzz there forever

And she smelled like blue violets
And Dixie Peach and the
Fragrance of fresh-washed sheets
Brought in from the sun and air

Mama was dressed for Sunday
In linen shoes

Mama patted the notes of the opening hymn shy and quick
Her voice fluttered over the mortuary fan
Her words accented sweet like sopped syrup on biscuits
hot with butter

"Deuteronomy second chapter, third verse:

You have compassed this way long enough Turn you northward"

Mama was dressed for Sunday

White lace on her collar
And crinkled lace on her sleeves
Sprinkle light in her hug
Then dance rhythms in our hearts
Throbbing spring evergreen

Mama was ready for Sunday

Like a sliver of lightning scratching across the sky,

THE HOLY GHOST BROKE OUT

And touched Sister Ruth, who fainted into the arms of Mama,
Who danced with the ghost, one hand behind her back
The other waving at something loose in the air

Her eyes closed
The ghost led her north
Led her on
Past any pain for arthritis
Past the limp in her leg
Past her flower garden strewed
Brilliant on the floor
And the neat bun of her hair
Unfolded and unlocked

Mama was there for Sunday

She danced stretching out the circle
And every time she tried
To sit down
The organ moaned
And screamed
The song reached out and held her
Then let her go

She'd almost made it to her seat
When the ghost sang

"YES"

With the organ
And that same song got her

A HALLELUJAH
Yanked itself out of her mouth
And trembled on my ears
I did not dare close them
A hallelujah splashed
All over the ceiling
And as she rose again to meet it

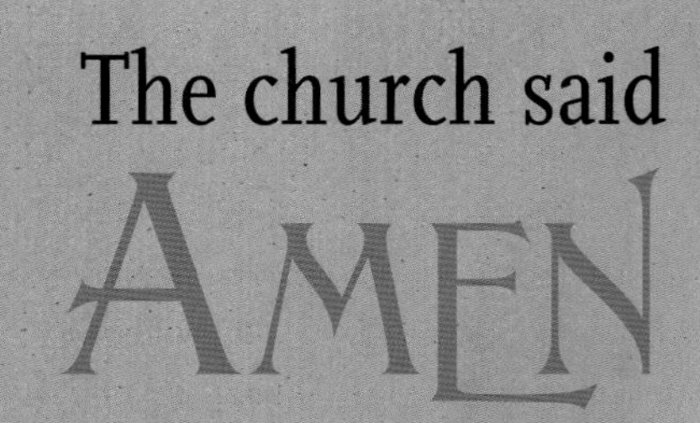
The church said
AMEN

And we are still shouting
On TV or alone in the shower
On the dance floor
In the glad-hall clubs
With strangers and friends
in the confetti rooms of celebration

Even now, when we dance like greased lightning,
Or move through spirit space, quick-stepping, hip-hopping
Finger-popping
Feet applauding planked floor
Echoing Africa, Africa, Africa

I can still see my mama's shout
I can still hear a myriad of
African musicians playing
On our souls, on our heartstrings
And we, still spirit-touched in
Our modern dance, move

Onward, upward, reaching
’Til we’re tracing back through time
The same steps, that same familiar . . .

AMEN!

AUTHOR'S NOTE

Shouting is the exhilarating, foot-tapping, hand-clapping echo of joy and faith. There is nothing more fascinating than watching people get caught up in the Holy Spirit, dancing on winged feet, propelled by spirited music, and skipping from one end of the church to the other.

There are all kinds of Shouting styles. In my church, there was brightly dressed Sister King, who whirled around in the aisles like a spinning top. Then there was Mother Boston's slow, humble dance; with her eyes closed and head bowed, she would rock back and forth in a prayerful sway. Once, I remember a visiting evangelist raising his arms toward heaven and running from aisle to aisle as if he were stepping on hot coals, joyously shouting, "Hallelujah!"

I have always longed to understand where Shouting came from. It was while I was miles away from home in Africa, for the International Festival of Arts, that I found the roots of Shouting—the roots of the holy dance.

In the Motherland, I inhaled the saffron smell of Africa while watching dancers from Egypt, Tanzania, Zimbabwe, Senegal, Ethiopia, Nigeria, and South Africa soar to the ebb and rise of drumbeats. I marveled at the lightning leaps of the seven-foot Tutsi dancers and the masterful musicians who made their instruments cry like leopards and trumpet like elephants! During my stay, I witnessed freedom unfurl in the surrendering dance of the body, in the incandescent spirit, mystical and awesome. I embraced the very soul of Africa.

When I left Africa, I flew with spirits dancing a holy dance on each wing of the plane. It seems that even through the terrors of the Middle Passage, our ancestors kept the beautiful memory of dance in their muscles, all the way to the shores of America.

Now, I rejoice again each time I see the Shout break out on a church house floor. You can almost see the happiness as it touches the hearts of the faithful, lifts up bowed heads with proud praise, and rises out of the smiles as a joyous Shout!

—Joyce Carol Thomas

ILLUSTRATOR'S NOTE

I have always been awed and inspired by the Bible, the church, its holy celebrations and the loving embrace of faith. To watch people release their fears, sorrows, and pain, and hand them over to God is remarkable. To experience God's blessings and grace through the Holy Spirit is definitely something to shout about!

Shouting is a powerful expression of faith and a true blessing that people experience differently. It is completely beautiful—there is so much going on between the Shouts and the holy dance.

I was inspired by Joyce Carol Thomas's words to show all the glory of the Shout. To capture the rapture of a Shout is almost impossible. It's something you need to see. My challenge has been to make the movement and excitement of a Holy Spirit visit come to life with color.

When I go to church, I see the Spirit *everywhere*. I see the Spirit in ladies' sparkling white gloves, in the lovely hats adorned with beautiful flowers, feathers and lace. I see praise to the Lord in the pressed suits and white shirts of little boys and their fathers. I see the lovely, flowing robes of the minister and the choir and see that faith has color and style and flows easily in the breeze. This dressing-up is a celebration, and it is the way we worship—the way we live.

Colorful layers of paint represent the powerful laying on of hands. The wiggle in my stroke shows the joyful movements of the holy dance. Listen closely as the bright splashes of paint sing the songs of the choir. Listen closely. You can almost hear the harmony of the hymns rising into the rafters and the trickle of joyful, forgiving tears as they cascade to the floor, and inspire the feet to find dance. There is such glory in the goodness of a Shout.

—Annie Lee